# MEETING A COUNTRY MAN

CONNOR WHITELEY

# DEDICATION

Thank you to all my readers without you I couldn't do what I love.

# CHAPTER 1
## 18th May 2023
### Canterbury, England

Ben Hamilton was so damn relieved as he sat down on the warm wooden picnic table in the middle of the immense green field of Kent University, because he was finally done with his university exams and he was now done with university.

At last.

He smiled as he watched an endless stream of other young university students walk down the long sloping concrete path down the hill, next to the field he was sitting in as they were all probably going home to pack up their houses, leave and run like hell away from this place.

Ben couldn't blame them at all. It was a wonderful, warm sunny day without a cloud in the sky, it was meant to heat up even more in the afternoon instead of cooling off and then despite how many parties were going on tonight to celebrate the end of third-year exams, he doubted anyone would really be going.

Everyone wanted to go home and enjoy the summer with their friends, family and loved ones.

Ben looked up at the massive white brick building at the top of the field that was dishing out great lunch, incredible milkshakes and the most delightful little vegan cupcakes he had ever had. Ben really enjoyed how the café made the aromas of mint, vanilla and rich coffee filled the air that left the great taste of coffee cake form on his tongue exactly how his grandmother used to make it.

Yet Ben was just glad to see his three best friends in the entire world walk down towards him.

He hadn't really seen Liz, Hunter and Caleb today. They hadn't met up for the exam because they were all panicking, they hadn't met up last night because they were all revising for the exam and he hadn't seen them for a few days. Especially with Hunter having girlfriend problems. Ben seriously felt sorry for him because dating problems were the last thing a student needed to worry about just before exams.

And Ben couldn't exactly say he liked Hunter's girlfriend anyway. She didn't exactly treat him too well and she was just foul.

Ben smiled at Hunter as he came over. He had always been cute, hot and just stunning with his broad shoulders and fit body, but Ben had accepted a long time ago that he wasn't going to get with Hunter.

Which wasn't really a bad thing he supposed when there were so many other hot guys about.

Caleb hugged Ben quickly before he sat next to him. Ben had to admit Caleb looked great in his jeans, white shirt and tan shoes that made him look incredible with his extreme height. His girlfriend was always lucky and she was always great to have around.

"How did you find it?" Liz asked.

Ben hugged her and he really couldn't understand how she could possibly be wearing a black dress in heat like this. It was stupid but he did love all of them.

"It wasn't as bad as I thought for a physics exam. I would have preferred a question on Thermal Dynamics instead of Pressure but I think it went fine," Ben said.

Liz looked into his eyes. "I thought Doctor Peterson said that Force would be on the exam paper so I focused so much on that. And it wasn't,"

Ben grinned at Hunter and Caleb and they just rolled their eyes.

"You actually think you did bad? That isn't possible you know and you got 80s and high 70s as grades for everything else. One exam isn't going to ruin you," Ben said.

"Exactly," Hunter said.

"True but I'm glad to be seeing the back of Mr Peterson," Liz said.

Ben laughed. He really wouldn't mind seeing the backside of Mr Peterson daily.

"Really Ben?" Caleb asked. "Are you that sexually frustrated you would want to see Mr Peterson's ass?"

Ben really didn't want to talk about that but Mr Peterson did have a great ass and he was actually a very good professor, something that was extremely hard to find these days.

"Anyway," Liz said sitting down on the picnic table, "what are the three of you doing tomorrow til Sunday?"

Ben shrugged. He didn't need to move out of his flat on campus for another month and he had been focusing so much on the exams he hadn't given after the exams any thought.

"Nothing," Ben said.

Everyone else nodded and Liz jumped up. "That is brilliant because I need all of you to come with me to the Cotswolds urgently,"

Ben just looked at Hunter and Caleb. "Remember the last time she did this and we were dragged off to Paris, why? Because someone wanted new shoes,"

"That didn't matter," Liz said knowing it was a lie.

"And what about the time we urgently had to go into Wales because someone wanted to see her favourite band?" Ben asked.

"You loved fucking that Welsh boy," Hunter said.

Ben grinned. That had been a great night.

But he had never been in the real countryside before and he really didn't see the appeal. Sure nature was beautiful, perfect and he had to admit that the pictures of the Cotswolds he had seen were stunning with its rolling hills, cute villages and perfect lifestyle.

But he was a city boy through and through he didn't want to go to the countryside, and it wasn't like there were going to be any cute men there to enjoy.

Yet as much as Ben hated it he would always do things for the friends he loved, and Liz was certainly one of those friends.

"Fine then," Ben said, "what about the time you urgently needed us to attend your Aunt's funeral that may I say was boring. Considering it was a ten-hour affair of boring speeches, awful music and your boring family,"

Liz placed her hands on her hips. "Why do you think I needed you there?"

Everyone laughed and then Hunter leant forward. "Why do you apparently need us to go?"

Ben shook his head as he realised that had to be the definition of famous last words because they were trapped now, and they were going wherever Liz said.

"We have to do to the Cotswold because my brother and his boyfriend are having a secret engagement party on Saturday night without our parents knowing. It's us lot, my brother and his boyfriend and their friends and my sister's going to be there too,"

Ben smiled. Liz definitely had a hot brother and

his boyfriend was flat out stunning too, but he had to admit Liz's sister was just brilliant to be around and she lived in Australia so it was rare for them to see her.

And Ben knew it wouldn't be a bad idea to talk to her because of the Masters programme he had applied to was in Sydney.

"Are we going then?" Liz asked.

Ben laughed because he would love nothing else than going to the Cotswolds for a secret engagement party for two beautiful men, for the best friends he loved and the Cotswolds were a beautiful place too.

## CHAPTER 2
### 19th May 2023

Bourton-On-The-Water, Cotswold, England

Max Dillion laid down on his perfectly soft white single bed as he waited for his best friend in the entire world, Elliot, to finally finish talking to his sister Quinn (the barwoman) and come up and tell him what was urgent.

He knew that Elliot and his boyfriend Phillip had got engaged because they were way too friendly and tactile for a small village like Bourton at the pub last night. But Max was so looking forward to actually hearing the news from Elliot directly.

Max looked at the wide open wooden door and still Elliot wasn't coming up the well-worn wooden stairs that he was fairly sure his parents, grandparents and even their grandparents had changed since the pub was founded over a hundred years ago, maybe even two hundred.

The dirty white walls of the small bedroom

weren't exactly much but Max really liked them. The entire bedroom was ancient, small and very intimate so whenever he was lucky enough to find a man who was also gay in somewhere as small as Bourton he could bring him back up here for a great night.

And as much as Max would have loved to go into the city or a town or just somewhere larger with more people and opportunities, he loved Bourton. It was beautiful, perfect and his family was here which with his mother having cancer was where he needed to be.

He couldn't imagine living or being anywhere else.

The hissing, whooshing and pumping of the pub's coffee machine (for the tourists) and the draught beer pumps were echoing up the stairs, and Max smiled as Elliot finally started coming up the old stairs.

Max sat up on his soft bed and just grinned as Elliot came through the wooden door in his blue denim shorts, grey t-shirt and white trainers that highlighted his hot body perfectly. Phillip was definitely a lucky man.

Max got up and hugged him like they always did. Elliot was a great hugger and Max couldn't lie there were some months when hugging his best friend was the only contact he actually had with another man.

He really needed to meet up with other men. Maybe he needed to download one of the dating apps or something but something had to be done.

"I have some news for you," Elliot said

nervously.

Max forced himself not to react, he already knew it but still.

"Me and Phillip are engaged!"

"Brilliant," Max shouted as he jumped on Elliot and hugged and gave him a small kiss on the cheek. "That's amazing. I couldn't be happier for you. Phillip's a lucky man,"

"Thanks mate and I have something else," Elliot said knowing Max had already had a thing for him. "My sister and her friends are coming for a party tomorrow but they're coming later today,"

Max nodded. He loved a good party even with a family as crazy as Elliot's.

"And I was wondering if you could help me get the house ready for them coming. Phillip's at work in Oxford so he can't help,"

"Sure I'd love too," Max said.

"Brilliant and there are three guys coming too,"

Max watched as Elliot quickly dashed down the stairs and he took that as Max should come round whenever he was free which he was all day. He wasn't working downstairs for hours yet and he was only working tomorrow morning.

He went downstairs and leant against the perfectly clean wooden bar where his tall wonderful sister was pulling pints for the regulars despite it being only 11 am. All the ten regulars were already sitting on their wooden round tables like they always did without fail.

Max knew each of them by name even from behind because the regulars always wore the same types of clothes. Like Mr and Mrs Jones with their 60s styles jumpers even in the stupid heat like today, or Mrs Appleton with her minty green dress that went out of fashion last century and the very cute Peter Ross who always came in with his mates and parents Friday morning after staying two nights with them before he went back to university in Oxford.

Max loved it here and this was his home and he just loved the community.

"When are you going to get married?" Quinn asked.

Max laughed. "When I can find a man to love and I'm only 22,"

Quinn finished pulling her pint and passed it to Mrs Oaks in her ugly grey dress and came over to him.

"You are 22 and you can find a great guy in a city or town or just somewhere that isn't here," Quinn said. "You know I love you and I just know you don't have a future here,"

Max shook his head. "I have you guys, a job here and I go do university online so I can still look after mum,"

Quinn kissed him on the head. "I'm 26 and I'm planning to leave as soon as possible. Just don't have any regrets,"

Max wanted to say something to her but then she went over to serve as a bunch of tourists that probably didn't know the difference between an IPA and Fosters.

Max just looked forward to that engagement party tomorrow.

But he couldn't help but feel like Elliot was trying to set him up with someone, and he really didn't like the idea of that.

He knew that hot sexy men didn't just come to the Cotswolds of all places looking for relationships. People only came here because they wanted to see the natural beauty, go hiking or feed the ducks if they came to Bourton.

They don't come here for relationships, love or anything like that.

But Max just didn't realise he was about to be proven seriously wrong.

# CHAPTER 3
19th May 2023
M40, England

Ben couldn't deny that as Liz drove them down the motorway that the M40 had to be one of the most awful motorways in the UK, because they were having to drive slow because of the awful traffic. Apparently there had been an accident up ahead but until that was sorted out they were stuck and sitting pretty.

Ben actually liked traffic at times because it meant he got to enjoy even more time with his amazing friends and it wasn't like the view was bad at all.

For as far as he could see there were green rolling hills filled with sheep, cows and wheat. The warm refreshing breeze carried the rich smells of nature, heat and coffee that everyone had seemed to buy at the last service station.

Ben enjoyed the breeze on his face as Liz opened

the windows even more and Ben couldn't deny that Liz's black Ford car-thingy (he was useless on cars) was so old that it was almost their age with it being made in 2004, he had to admit it was a great little thing to drive about.

And Liz was a great driver considering it was the rest of her family that made the insurance industry worth billions of pounds.

Ben really couldn't remember the last week Liz hadn't mentioned a story about one of her relatives getting into a car crash, accident or bump. It just seemed that the entire family were nightmares and Ben was really glad that all of them had a pack with each other.

If anyone from Liz's family tried to be nice and offered to drive them somewhere, another one had to save them.

And Ben was pretty sure that pack had saved their lives more times than he cared to admit.

Ben was glad that Liz hadn't asked about him missing the city, but the further towards their destination they got, the more he was slowly (extremely slowly) starting to warm up to the idea of the countryside.

It was beautiful after all.

Hunter's and Caleb's snoring filled up the back of the car and Ben smiled at how his best friends had done clubbing last night with their girlfriends to make up for spending the weekend away from them. From what they had said before they both passed out, it sounded like a great night but Ben had no idea about clubbing.

He had never ever done it and he didn't intend to. It just wasn't his thing. His idea of a fun night was spending it with friends without alcohol or loud music and thousands of strangers.

"You're going to love this engagement party," Liz said. "It is going to be brilliant and I am so looking forward to seeing Lucy again,"

"Me too," Ben said, but not daring to mention how he wanted to talk to her because of his Masters.

"You know she has a spare room and everything," Liz said knowing Ben was nervous about Australia. "And you know she loves you and would love to have you,"

Ben smiled. He loved how Liz just knew him so well and that was probably why they had been friends since they met in secondary school. She was so kind, helpful and brilliant but it was annoying at times.

"You aren't mad, are you about me moving?" Ben asked.

Liz laughed as the traffic slowly started moving. "Don't be silly. You have to do what you need to do in this life and Australia will suit you perfectly and you might as well travel a little with your degree,"

Ben wanted to hug or something because she really did know him too well. He knew that once he was working with a job and everything then he wouldn't give the UK a second thought because the flight was expensive as hell and if someone was going to travel all that way then you really had to go there for months at a time.

And if Ben had a full-time job then that wasn't going to happen at all.

"And with you in Australia and Lucy there, then I'm going to *have* to visit," Liz said grinning.

"I would like that," Ben said and he meant every word of it.

"And I would love you to marry an Australia man," Liz said knowing how Ben loved her, "and then you could always hear that sexy accent,"

Ben grinned and sank back a little into his chair because she was definitely right. Australian men did have a sexy accent and they were hot as well with their fit, tanned bodies.

"So what's happening when we get there?" Ben asked.

Liz laughed as she probably realised she hadn't explained anything yet. "We're going to a place called Bourton-On-The-Water. My brother and his boyfriend have a large house there and that's where we're staying and then tomorrow night the party is going to be held there too,"

"Nice," Ben said. He had no idea how big this house was but he trusted Liz and even if it was a little small he knew it would still be a great night because he was with friends, family and there to celebrate a gay engagement.

Something he would absolutely love to do himself one day.

Little did Ben know that be a lot more likely than he thinks.

# CHAPTER 4
## 19th May 2023
### Bourton-On-The-Water, Cotswolds, England

Max leant against the wonderfully warm Cotswold limestone wall of the house as he smiled at Elliot who was pacing up and down the long gravel driveway with hedges rising up around the front garden. He would have loved to have owned a house like this.

Every time he came round, which wasn't a lot with his university, his pub shifts and him hiking about the Cotswolds, he just couldn't believe how beautiful the house was. The front garden was the size of most people's backyards in the town, it had an apple tree, a child's swing and three beds of roses.

It was so nice and relaxing to look at and the house itself was stunning. Max couldn't deny that the pub his family lived in was great and it seriously had its own charm, but the sandy yellow limestone of his place was great.

But it was the ancient black single-panel windows that really did it for Max. He felt like he was looking at something in the past instead of the tourist-infested village.

Max straightened his cargo shorts, blue polo shirt and rose gold bracelet as Elliot looked like his sister was right round the corner. She couldn't have been given how silent this end of the village was away from the tourists but it was good seeing Elliot a little nervous.

He was normally such a confident guy that never seemed to be upset or concerned about anything. Max was relieved to see Elliot could be nervous about something, it just helped to remind Max that Elliot was human after all.

"Should I get her something from the bakery?" Elliot asked.

Max laughed because Elliot had to be seriously panicking. Everyone in Burton knew never ever to go to the bakery at this time of day during tourist season. It was always safer and better to email or write to Frank and his family, order something and have them deliver it personally.

It was so, so much quicker that way and it allowed Frank to focus on the tourists which would actually allow him to retire. Not that he ever would.

And it was that spirit and passion and joy that Bourton was filled with that Max loved so much. He didn't want to leave them but he couldn't help but focus on what Quinn had mentioned earlier.

He wanted a boyfriend, he wanted to explore the world and he wanted to know what life was like beyond the Cotswolds, but he just couldn't leave his mum and the family pub.

"Here they are," Elliot said smiling as a tiny ancient Ford Fiesta drove onto the gravel and almost killed Elliot where he stood.

Max wouldn't have minded that and at least that way the entire family could live up to their reputation. Max just didn't have the heart to tell Elliot that there was a Cotswolds-wide warning system in place that if someone knew Elliot was on the road they had to post on the social media group so everyone knew not to travel or to be extremely careful on the roads.

Max went over to the driver's side and hugged Liz as she got out the car. He could definitely tell that they were family, they were happy and had the same mouth, nose and ears but Liz really was more beautiful.

"Hi mate," two men said as they got out the car and shook Max's hand.

Max smiled slightly. They were certainly hot and fit and very easy on the eyes, but Max could just tell they were straight and both of them probably had the girlfriends to prove it.

"Go away woman," one of the men said denying a call.

Max shook his head, he didn't like being proven right but it always made things easier later on. "Girlfriend problems?"

"Yeah mate," the man said. "Do you have a girlfriend?"

"No," Max said grinning to himself. The very last thing he would ever do was get a girlfriend.

"Good, they are the biggest pains you will never have. Do not get one under any circumstances," the man said.

"Good being such a downer Hunter," Liz said. "I'm sure there are tons of nice girls in the Cotswolds for such a cute man like you,"

Max smiled but even though he knew she didn't know he was gay, it always annoyed him when someone just presumed he was perfectly straight and wanted to date them like no tomorrow.

"Come on Ben," Liz said as her brother helped her get the luggage from the boot.

Max watched as a man jumped out the passenger side and… holy fuck.

Max fell forward a little and just had to force himself to grab the bonnet of the car before he collapsed to the ground as he stared at the Greek God of a man walking towards him.

Max's mouth went dry instantly as he focused on the man's smooth handsome face that looked like it belonged on a model more than a mere mortal man, and his slim sexy, well-toned body looked so damn wonderful in that loose orange t-shirt that made Max really want to run his hands down it. And Max seriously couldn't tear his eyes away from the man's great ass he stopped, turned around and answered a question from Hunter for a moment.

Max had no idea asses could be that perfect but then Max noticed the hot man was walking towards him again and he was grinning.

He wasn't frowning, he wasn't smiling, he was grinning at him. Max was stunned by his sexy grin and pearly white perfect smile.

Max's wayward parts flared to life and he instantly knew this was going to be an extremely hard weekend.

In more ways than one.

# MEETING A COUNTRY MAN

# CHAPTER 5
## 19th May 2023
### Bourton-On-The-Water, Cotswolds, England

Ben just stood there as he stared at the flat out stunning man in front of him. The Angel couldn't have been any older than him at 22 but Ben just couldn't believe that such a beautiful man actually existed in the first place. His entire mind was a chaotic blur of the hot Angel as they both smiled at each other.

Ben really loved the man's hot fit body that his tight polo shirt highlighted perfectly. Ben seriously didn't care there were no muscles or anything even remotely well-defined under that Polo shirt but he could just tell how fit the man was without any body fat.

And Ben absolutely loved the man's smooth handsome face with his strong manly jawline, cute little nose and stunning golden brown eyes that Ben was certain could only belong to an Angel.

But Ben definitely loved the Angel's beautiful black curls that framed his handsome face perfectly and Ben so badly wanted to go over to the Angel and brush those soft, seductive curls away from his perfect face.

Ben hadn't even noticed his wayward parts flaring to life unless Liz subtly gestured him to cover up his man parts.

Ben didn't care as he went over to the Angel and grinned at him like an idiot.

He really could be a country boy if it meant he got to spend time with this divine angel.

"Hi," Ben said before his throat and voice seemed to die on him and he couldn't even begin to think of anything smart, witty or remotely intelligent to say.

The Angel seemed to be having a similar problem.

Ben loved how the Angel bit his lower lip and his throat seemed to be shaking as much as he was. The Angel was so damn cute.

"Ben," Liz said coming to stand next to him. "His name is Ben and he clearly finds you very hot,"

Ben just looked at Liz. As much as he loved her as a friend, how dare she interrupt him and make the cute weird. Not that it wasn't unweird without her comments.

Thankfully the Angel laughed and he extended his hand. "I'm Max and it's very nice to meet you Ben,"

Ben shook the stunning Angel's soft, smooth hand and he was shocked by the strength, warmth and sheer voltage pulsing through him with the handshake. Ben made sure the car bonnet wasn't too far behind him in case he needed to collapse against it.

Max could seriously shake hands.

Ben wanted to hug and kiss him right there and then but he couldn't, not with his friends and Elliot just there.

After a few moments Ben sadly broke the handshake and he forced himself to admire the rather average house he was going to be staying in for the weekend. The house wasn't that bad with its Cotswold sandy yellow limestone, ancient windows and gravel driveway that was mostly sheltered from street view but it was nothing compared to Max.

Ben was sure that the entire house could be made from gold and diamonds and rubies and it would still be ugly compared to Max.

"I guess we better go inside," Max said.

"I don't know I rather like the view out here," Ben said, wanting the ground to swallow him whole as soon as he said such a silly and romantic thing.

Max grinned a little. "Really? A few moments ago you could barely talk to me and now you're flirting with me. What else you got in that pretty mouth of yours?"

Ben felt himself blush. He couldn't believe he was already flirting with such a good, perfect Angel of

28

a man but he forced himself to remember that he couldn't do a relationship. Not with him starting his Masters in Australia in September.

It just wasn't fair on Max, but that didn't mean he couldn't have a little fun this weekend and make sure his feelings didn't develop any more than a mere hot hookup.

Ben nodded to himself because that was the perfect plan.

He followed Max inside the rather okay house.

A few moments later, he was sitting on a very old and ugly red sofa in a great-looking, very traditional Cotswold living room with immensely thick black beams running across the ceiling and walls, the white walls were uneven and covered in family photos (including some of Liz as a child) and the ancient handcrafted coffee table all of them were sitting around looked like it was going to break at any moment.

Ben really hoped it wouldn't break at all.

The house smelt delightful with hints of vanilla, warming ginger and sweet caramel that clung to the air as Elliot bought out a plate of cookies for all of them to enjoy. Ben took one bit of the explosively flavourful biscuits and he thought he had died and gone to heaven.

It was sheer magical baking perfection.

Ben took a large mug of tea from Elliot as he finally sat down and everyone except Hunter and Caleb sat there with a mug of tea. Ben smiled at

Hunter declined yet another call from his girlfriend.

"Why don't you just talk to her?" Liz asked.

"What's going on?" Max asked.

Ben just smiled as he spoke. His voice was so perfect, smooth and beautiful that Ben so badly wanted him to keep talking so he didn't have to listen to anyone but him.

He couldn't believe how much he liked Max but there was just something about him that made Ben want to spend more time with him, get to know him better and just *be* with him.

"My girlfriend's panicking that once I start my physics Masters at Kent in September I'm going to leave her because she isn't continuing her studies. She did Business Management and she's going straight into work," Hunter said.

"Would leaving her be such a bad thing?" Ben asked, half meaning it.

Hunter smiled. "Yes because I love her and she loves me. We just need to have a serious conversation that we will still be together but I don't know how to talk about it with her. And even worse now she wants to spend every single second of the day with me in case we break up,"

Elliot took a large sip of his tea. "Just talk to her. Me and Phillip only lasted this long by talking about our troubles,"

Ben grinned at Max when Elliot said that and he was surprised that Max smiled back. He really liked the idea of a long-term relationship with a hot, sexy man and he really wanted that to happen with Max, as impossible as that was.

"Maybe you're right," Hunter said. "I'll talk to her later on,"

Ben knew that meant he wasn't going to talk to her but he had tried to help Hunter so much and he realised now that sometimes he just couldn't help someone until they were ready to help themselves. It was a shame because Hunter was a hot guy but still, until Hunter was ready there was nothing he could do.

Elliot downed his tea in one. "You guys want to see your rooms?"

Ben leant over to Max. "Do you have a room?"

Max laughed like a cute little schoolboy and shook his head. "I live in a pub in the village,"

Ben smiled. "A cute man that lives in a pub surrounded by pints. Do you have any flaws?"

Max laughed and Liz shook her head as she overheard but Ben couldn't deny the more he learnt about Max the more he was liking him.

He just had a feeling keeping his feelings about this as a hookup was going to be a lot harder than he ever wanted to admit.

# CHAPTER 6
## 19th May 2023

Bourton-On-The-Water, Cotswolds, England

"Oh, this is wonderful Ellie," Liz said.

Max laughed as he saw Elliot gently elbow his sister in the ribs as he led them into a very old bedroom that Max hadn't seen before. The wooden door was so old, cracked and worn that Max had always believed this was a storage room or something, it had never occurred to him that this was a bedroom of all things.

He leant on the warm wooden doorframe as Elliot went to the centre of the small bedroom with sandy yellow limestone walls that kept the bedroom surprisingly cool and he gestured to the two small single bedrooms that Max was sure came from the last century.

He could tell just by looking at them that they didn't have any back support, any real springs and he wouldn't have been surprised if the entire bed was made from duck feathers. The bed might have been comfortable but after a few days, Max knew that Liz and sexy Ben would have bad backs at the very least.

Max smiled as he realised that might not be that bad if it meant he had to massage Ben's fit perfect body to help release some of the stress caused by the bed.

All he could do as Ben put his luggage and travel bag on the slightly dusty bed was how perfect Ben was, how his slim fit body moved so artfully and elegantly like he had been born to walk around a house as old and elegant as this one, and Ben was just so damn cute.

Max rubbed his hands on his shorts as he realised he was badly sweating, something he had never ever done before. He actually didn't understand why he was doing a lot of what he was doing around Ben. He never normally flirted so openly with a man he just met, he certainly didn't watch them like a stalker and he never got sweaty around guys.

He just wasn't that sort of man.

Max felt his stomach fill with butterflies as Ben smiled as him and Liz started unpacking her things into the small brown chest of drawers at the foot of her bed. He couldn't deny the design was stunning with little birds, animals and houses carved into the wood of the chest.

It was functional art, his favourite type of art.

"This is such a beautiful room," Ben said. "You know how lucky you are to live here,"

Max grinned. He never got bored of tourists saying that to him and he loved it even more when Ben said it. Maybe if he really loved it then he might even want to stay, that would be great.

"I can show you all the sites if you want," Max said failing to hide how desperate he was to spend more time with Ben.

Liz laughed. "I thought you two would get on well. I bet before the night is over you two would have kissed,"

Max pretended to look offended but Ben laughed and blew him a little kiss as a joke. Max was surprised how his wayward part flared to life at the sight of Ben's large, soft lips blowing him a perfect little kiss.

All Max wanted to do was go over there, kiss those wonderful lips and just enjoy Ben. Of course he knew Ben was leaving on Sunday so they only had two days together but he was more than determined to make every single moment count with such a beautiful man.

"My sister's coming down in a few hours," Liz said.

"That's if she doesn't get into a car accident first," Max said smiling.

Liz nodded. "True, true,"

Ben took out a slightly shiny black shirt that Max couldn't help but grin at. He didn't doubt for a moment that Ben would look perfect, sexy and just damn divine in that shirt that would highlight how fit he really was.

Max forced himself to focus on other things. He couldn't keep being obsessed with Ben, he didn't want Ben to think he was a creep or something, but he had just never seen such a hot man before that was also gay.

There was a massive difference there.

Max went over to him and sat on the bed. He almost jumped at how it almost swallowed him whole, this was definitely a duck feather bed from the last century.

"What's Canterbury like? I've never left the Cotswolds so I don't really know what a city is like, or much of a town for that matter," Max said.

Ben gave him a mischievous grin. "So you're a little country boy falling for a city man?"

Max laughed and buried his face in his hands. He wouldn't quite put it like that but it was pretty close to the truth.

And the truth was he wanted Ben so badly.

"I'm sorry," Ben said, "I honestly don't flirt this much normally, and can I say something a little cheesy or something?"

"I can promise you he is crap at flirting normally," Liz said taking out a very nice long white dress.

"Sure," Max said really not wanting Ben to ever stop talking.

"I think there's something about you that I really like so that's why I'm flirting. Sorry if I'm being too strong or something," Ben said.

Max touched his arm and almost gasped at the sheer heat, passion and lust that flowed through him. He never wanted this touch to end.

"No it's fine, honest," Max said. "I know what you mean about there's something about us or just you. Yeah, I don't flirt either,"

Elliot poked his head back through the door. "But there's a difference Max, you don't flirt because there are no gay guys to flirt with in the Cotswolds. Ben doesn't flirt because he's just awful at it,"

Max wasn't sure why Ben was blushing but he had a little feeling that there was some history between Ben and Elliot, not that he could blame the two men at all.

But all Max wanted to do was spend more and more time with beautiful Ben.

"Max don't you have a pub shift in ten minutes?" Elliot asked.

Max rolled his eyes because that sadly meant he would be away from Ben and that was the very last thing he ever wanted to do.

# CHAPTER 7
19th May 2023

Bourton-On-The-Water, Cotswolds, England

Ben flat out couldn't believe how cute, beautiful and angelic Max was as he sat on a very rocky little wooden table in the pub that Max's family owned. After catching up with Elliot, how the proposal happened and making sure that Hunter and Caleb were settled in too, Ben was really glad that going to the pub had been the next great idea.

He really liked the old-world vibe of the pub because it's dirty white walls were covered in pictures of the Cotswolds and Bourton through the ages and there were at least five pictures a decade. The large ancient windows were wide open allowing a delightfully warm breeze to past through as the sun slowly started to set in the distance over some rolling hills Ben could see, and this place was just perfect.

Ben could see there were at least three rows of small round wooden tables were tourists and regulars and people from all over the Cotswolds were sitting, laughing and just enjoying life.

He noticed that a lot of them were drinking IPA and other local ales, but he wasn't a fan of those drinks. He had always preferred a gin or a nice glass of red wine which he had already noticed some of the other locals had turned their nose up at him.

He didn't care because he was still supporting the local economy, he got his drink and Ben got to watch the perfect young man he was getting more and more feelings for.

Ben watched Max as he moved so gracefully, artfully and elegantly behind the massive wooden bar covered in beer and spirit bottles with large draught beer pumps that had a great selection considering how tiny Bourton was. Ben could understand why Max liked it here, he was laughing with the regulars, helping tourists and just being a wonderful friendly guy.

Ben didn't know how Max did it, because he had done some bar work at the various university pubs and cafes and he was awful at it. He didn't have the friendly appearance to drunk students, demeanour and ability to tell bar jokes that so many students wanted to hear.

"He's single you know," Elliot said sitting next to Ben and Liz leant forward across the table.

Ben looked at Hunter and Caleb who were sipping their local ales and smiled so Ben was fully aware that everyone wanted to know the "low down" on what he thought of Max.

"There's nothing to tell," Ben said knowing he was lying to himself. "Max is a beautiful man that seems perfect in every way but remember, we couldn't ever be together,"

"Why not?" Elliot said like that was the most stupid thing he had ever heard.

"Because I'm going to Australia in September so what would we do? Have a summer fling, get involved and I would shatter his beautiful heart come September?" Ben asked.

Hunter shook his head. "But you like him a lot, you just said that and shouldn't you at least give it a chance,"

Ben laughed as Hunter's phone went again and he declined the call from his girlfriend.

"Should I really be taking dating advice from you Hunt?" Ben asked taking a wonderful sip of red wine and allowed the full-bodied notes with hints of fruity sweetness linger on his tongue for a few moments.

"Probably not," Hunter said, "but my point is clear. You like the guy and come on, what did you say to the guy earlier?"

Liz laughed. "Oh yeah, you can give him some big city sex education,"

Ben took a massive sip of red wine. He knew that line was going to bite him in the ass as soon as he said it, now he really regretted it. But that was the weird thing about how perfect Max was, Ben never would have flirted or said something that strange to a man before.

Yet Max was making him want to say and do so many strange, crazy, mind-blowing things.

"Deny it then," Liz said. "Say that you don't want Max and we'll stop bothering you,"

Ben just looked at Max as he laughed with two female tourists as he finished pouring them their pints and he couldn't say that. Max was so cute and handsome that there wasn't anything he would rather do than be with him or at least try.

Ben turned to Elliot. "When does Max get off shift?"

"Well that is the question," Elliot said, "normally about 12 am but this is tourist season and some tourists love to drink on a Friday night so about 2 am,"

Ben shrugged. "Fine then. I am staying here until 2 am so I can spend time with him,"

Liz mockingly threw her arms in the air like she was completely defeated. "But that means I'm wrong about you two kissing tonight,"

Ben leant over the table and held her hand for a moment. "Last time I checked night ended at 5 when the sun rose, not at midnight. We might get to kiss before 5 if I play my cards right,"

Caleb choked on his IPA. "Just do me a favour please that if you two do end up having sex, don't tell me about it. I don't want to know that my best friend who hasn't had a boyfriend in years is getting more than me with a girlfriend,"

Ben mockingly cheered to Caleb but he couldn't deny that he was surprised Caleb and his girlfriend weren't active in that department. Not that it really mattered because Ben knew that relationships weren't built on sex and there was more to a relationship than sex, because relationships were built on love, respect and real interest in each other.

And Ben had to admit he was a lot more interested in Max than he ever wanted to admit.

# CHAPTER 8

20th May 2023

Bourton-On-The-Water, Cotswolds, England

Max was so glad that the shift had been amazing, fun and his jaw actually hurt so much from laughing. He really did love tourist season because there were always great tourists that came into the pub and he got to hear some great stories about what the world was like outside of the Cotswolds.

As he finished wiping down the warm sticky wooden bar after some regulars had accidentally slipped their drinks, Max had loved hearing one story from a woman all the way from York about how massive the historic city was with the Vikings, night life and sheer amount of people.

And as Max just stood there behind the bar in the sheer silence without any warm breeze now that he had shut the windows and the aromas of spices, beer and whisky lingering in the air, he couldn't help but feel like he did want more than this place.

He wasn't sure why he had never gone travelling, why he hadn't travelled more than Oxford and the Cotswolds, and why he didn't have dreams about leaving this place forever like his sister was planning too.

Max supposed it was partly because he loved his family way too much to leave them. He loved his family more than anything and they had always been there for him when he came out, when he was bullied and when his boyfriends dumped him in the past.

His family was his everything.

A quiet snoring sound filled the bar and Max noticed in the corner there was a very hot man snoring away to himself on a table. And Max just shook his head as he finished up, turned off the lights and went over to beautiful Ben.

Max just looked at the utterly stunning man who was sound asleep snoring on the wooden table in front of him, and Max was realising now just had tired he was. He had already wiped down the table where Ben and everyone had been at, and somehow he had missed the most perfect stunning man he had ever met sleeping there.

"Aren't you done yet son?" Max's father asked as he gave into the pub from the stairs.

Max smiled at his father who was wearing a very thin black dressing gown that his parents seemed to use equally. Max wasn't sure who the growing gown actually belonged too.

"Yeah dad I was just finishing wiping up and

closing down,"

"Who's the fella?" his father asked. "New boyfriend?"

Max laughed. "I wish. He's called Ben, a friend of Elliot's sister and he's beautiful, isn't he?"

His father shrugged. "I have no idea son if he's beautiful or not, but I can sort of understand why you think that. Is he drunk or something? Do we need to call Elliot or anyone to come and get him?"

Max was so tempted to say no because he would have loved nothing more to simply drag a very tired Ben upstairs into his own bed, even if it was just to make sure Ben was safe, warm and cared for tonight.

But he couldn't ask his dad if that was okay not with his mother needed all the rest she could.

"You could take him upstairs you know," his father said knowing what his son really wanted. "It's okay and I wouldn't mind. Sometimes I think you forget sonny boy just how thick these walls are. Me and your mother are still active adults,"

Max coughed and crossed his legs out of instinct, he didn't care what his parents got up to but he seriously didn't want to know or even have that awful image inside his head.

"But I would just say son that you check if he's drunk or not first. If so make sure you take a bucket up," his father said going back upstairs.

Max nodded and whispered that he loved his father as he went over to Ben and gently tapped him on the shoulder.

After a few moments Ben slowly woke up and Max simply stared into those rich stunningly perfect eyes that were the only thing he wanted to look into. Ben was so fit and perfect and then he realised Ben was actually wearing that slightly shiny black shirt.

Max smiled as he realised just how tired he was and how insanely busy today had been at the pub. He really should have noticed something as hot as that shirt but he was tired and he wanted to go to bed, and he wanted to tear his eyes away from Ben's fit insanely hot body.

He couldn't.

"Are you drunk?" Max asked.

"Do I look drunk? I only had two glasses of wine and then I was on Diet coke all night for you,"

Max sat on the table and he moaned in pleasure when Ben placed a firm and seductive hand on his thigh. "What do you mean for me?"

"I can't exactly get to know you, can I, if I'm wasted and drunk as hell," Max said. "Are you free now?"

Max wanted to stay up and talk and do so many amazing things to this hot sexy man that was clearly trying to impress him and be with him, but he couldn't deny that he didn't have the brain power for this.

"Come up stairs with me, let's sleep on it and we can talk all day tomorrow I promise," Max said knowing exactly how lame that was.

"I would love to, really I would I'm just glad to

be here," Ben said not wanting Max to think he was being lame. "And I promise I won't try anything tonight,"

Max shrugged and he took Ben's hand in his and pulled him up the stairs into his bedroom because he actually wanted to test his father's theory.

How thick were these walls?

# CHAPTER 9
20th May 2023

Bourton-On-The-Water, Cotswolds, England

When Ben woke up at midday he couldn't believe how great he felt but he was surprised that the duck feather bed felt so supportive, strange and like a very modern bed. Liz had told him years ago when she was doing an optional module in The American West history about how awful duck feather beds were, so why was this one so great?

Ben enjoyed as the softness of the bedsheets and duvet took his weight and they felt so smooth, modern and soft that he couldn't believe how refreshed he felt. It was such a great change compared to his little flat at the university accommodation, but the ceiling was off.

He could have sworn that earlier when he had been unpacking his things that ceiling of the bedroom was white plaster but this one had large black beams running through it.

Ben rolled over and he gasped as he saw the smiling beautiful handsome face of Max as he covered up his body with a bedsheet.

He made sure that he was clothed and Ben was more than glad he was fully clothed and nothing had been done to him at all. The last thing he wanted was to have sex with such an angelic man only to not remember it.

"Relax, we didn't have sex or kiss or anything," Max said knowing how badly Ben wanted to remember it. "As soon as you and me gave into my bedroom your head hit the pillow and you fell asleep,"

Ben sat up and he just shook his head. He had wanted a great time with hot, sexy Max to enjoy him, kiss him and make sure Liz's prediction came true but it hadn't happened. He had been way too tired.

"I'm sorry?" Ben said more of a question than a statement.

Max laughed and kissed him. Ben moaned in pleasure as he tasted how amazing Max's soft, full smooth lips were against his. The kiss was passionate, loving and tender.

Ben gripped onto the bedsheets as the entire world spun around them, Ben's heart pounded in his chest and his stomach was about to burst full of butterflies.

"Don't say sorry," Max said breaking the kiss. "You're perfect,"

Ben kissed him again and again and then a

woman knocked on the door. He had no idea who the woman was or why she was here but she only could have been a few years older than Max, and her jeans and red t-shirt highlighted a slim figure.

He still had no clue who she was.

As Max got out of the bed and Ben was hopeful Max was naked but sadly he was wearing shorts on so Ben rolled his eyes. He so badly wanted to see his lower body but just seeing Max bare chested was great.

Ben focused on all the smooth, slim muscles that moved so carefully as Max walked and Ben couldn't deny that Max was so damn beautiful.

"Quinn, this is Liz's friend Ben," Max said, "and no before you ask we didn't have sex and have only just kissed,"

Ben laughed as Quinn rolled her eyes.

"I told you before," Quinn said, "when you guess what I want to ask it isn't any fun. And I came to ask what happened to the extra three cases of dark ale we got on Thursday. A bunch of tourists want it,"

"Basement third shelf on the left hand side," Max said.

Quinn gave her brother a quick kiss on the cheek and rushed back down the stairs.

Ben just grinned like the little schoolboy he was right now watching such a beautiful angel just walk around topless in the bedroom. It was nice seeing how Max was with his sister, Ben couldn't say he was overly close with his sister and brother but they all loved each other.

Yet it was clear as day that Quinn and Max treasured each other, and that was great to see.

"You love her don't you?" Ben asked sitting up perfectly straight.

"Yeah, I love my whole family really. It's probably why I don't really leave the Cotswolds really, because I have to help Quinn with the pub, my dad helps with shifts when he can but he has to look after mum a lot. She has cancer,"

Ben didn't know how to react at all. He had lost his grandmother a few years back to lung cancer and it was awful. Cancer was a cold, calculating evil thing that Ben really wanted destroyed, but until that happened it would continue to claim people.

Ben got off the bed and just hugged Max. It was all he could think of doing, but it was sad that Max had never left the Cotswolds before. There was a massive world outside and whilst the Cotswolds were beautiful (and somewhere he still needed to explore) there were plenty of other beautiful places too.

"Thanks for the hug," Max said. "You know I am free until the party tonight. I could show you about, show you the sites and show you a very, very, secret spot I took a boy in the past,"

Ben laughed as he felt Max lightly trace a finger down his spine and towards his bum. "I don't know," he said smiling. "I might have to show my big city moves on you,"

Max shook his head. "I'm not as much of an

innocent country boy as you imagine,"

Ben laughed and just kissed beautiful Max again because they both knew Max really was an innocent country boy that didn't know a thing about the wider world.

And as Max broke the sweet kiss to put a top on, Ben forced himself not to frown as he realised that there would be no chance in hell Max would ever come with him to Australia.

So this well and truly was a weekend fling and it could never ever be anything more.

A realisation that utterly killed Ben inside.

# CHAPTER 10
## 20th May 2023

Bourton-On-The-Water, Cotswolds, England

As much as Max wanted to show Ben the main part of Bourton including its stunning river, small yellow bridges and ducks that people fed like no tomorrow, he really wanted to take him the long way (and more private way) through the beautiful rolling hills and fields that went around Burton first.

Max held Ben's smooth and warm and slightly sweaty hand as they both walked along a long tarmacked road going like a steep hill with lustrous green grass and sheep and cows on either side.

He focused on a little dirty white sheep as she came over and rested her head on the flint wall as they walked past. She started making a ton of noise and Max couldn't help but wonder if she was talking to him.

Max shook the silly idea away. The damn heat was probably messing with his brain.

The air smelt great with hints of nature, cows and sheer heat as the boiling hot sun beamed down on them. Max loved days like this because it made the hike more challenging and the heat made the exploring even more worth it.

The thick group of trees a good few hundred metres away made Max smile at Ben who was looking a little tired, and he supposed that city boys just didn't hike much. That was probably another reason why he loved the Cotswolds.

There was nothing else to do but hike and just enjoy the incredible nature all around him.

"So tell me about yourself?" Ben asked as if this was a first date.

Max frowned a little. He had no idea what men normally said on a first date or something, he had only had a few but Ben had probably been with hundreds of men from university and the cities.

What could Max offer him?

"I mainly work at the family pub, do my uni work online and look after mum. What about you?" Max asked stepping over a crack in the road.

"Oh cool. How do you find online uni and what you study? I do physics," Ben said.

Max smiled at how excited, passionate and thrilled Ben sounded at his choice of subject. Max wished he had the same undying passion for his own degree.

"Online's okay. It allows me to fit it around bar shifts, when I need to look after mum and it means I get to stay local. But I do kinda wish I had the *real* university experience,"

Ben wrapped an arm around Max's waist. He loved that feeling.

"I study, don't laugh, history and historical site conservation. It sounds silly but I love the Cotswolds and it's natural beauty and there are some brilliant ruins around here that are under constant threat from buildings, erosion and the weather," Max said.

Ben kissed him. "That sounds brilliant,"

Max stopped and couldn't understand if he was joking or not. No one had ever had that reaction before, even his own family thought he was wasting his time and a lot of the time even he thought that. He just did the online degree because he wanted an option, any option to leave the Cotswolds one day.

If only he could get up the courage to actually do it.

"I mean it. I really do think that sounds useful," Ben said knowing Max couldn't tell if he was joking. "We need to protect historical sites because we need to learn from the past and that only happens if the sites exist,"

Max gave him a deep passionate kiss. Ben seriously was amazing and he so badly wanted to see him beyond the weekend, and chances are that would easily happen. It wasn't like he was leaving the UK or doing his Masters in another country.

"Why did you think I was joking or something?" Ben asked.

Max kept walking and waved as one of the pub regulars drove past in their brown pick up truck.

"Because even I don't know if it's worth my time some days. I love history, I love conservation but sometimes I wish I had some uni friends to talk with," Max said.

"Don't you have a chance to make friends on your online course?"

"Yeah but they live in cities and work full-time jobs and have families to look after. They have real reasons to do an online degree, I just, you know, don't feel like I fit in,"

Max stopped as Ben pushed him gently against the flint wall so he had to sit down.

"You are incredible, great and a wonderful person. Don't you ever believe you aren't good enough for someone or something. So what you don't live in a massive city and you don't have many life experiences, I still really like the man I'm looking at,"

Max smiled and kissed Ben again. "You're pretty wonderful too,"

A sheep headbutted his ass.

Max surged forward.

Ben started weeing himself laughing and Max playfully hit him over the head but he really did appreciate the words. No one had ever said something that kind, romantic and just nice to him before.

Max knew that he should have tried harder to make more friends online, he should have tried to be more social in Burton but everything was just so busy. And he might have got on great with all the regulars, young and old, but it didn't make up for a lack of real friends.

And as him and Ben kept hiking along the long road he couldn't help but feel like his time in Bourton was coming to a close and that he needed to move on.

Not so much like Quinn had wanted (even though he hated his sister being right) but because he really hoped that Ben would want to stay with him and they could explore the wider world together.

Little did Max know just how wider Ben's world would be come September.

# CHAPTER 11
## 20th May 2023

Bourton-On-The-Water, Cotswolds, England

Ben was having the absolute best time of his life as he went hand in hand with his sexy angel Max along the massively long little river that went through the heart of Bourton. And he flat out couldn't believe he had missed with stunning beauty yesterday.

Everything was so stunning as he focused on the shallow little river filled with crystal clear water allowing him to see the peddles, rocks and the occasional broken brick at the bottom of the river as the icy cold water flowed quickly downstream.

He was really impressed that every so often, maybe every twenty or so metres, there were little bridges made from the sandy yellow Cotswold limestone that the entire area seemed obsessed with.

Ben smiled as he saw tourists pose on different bridges as they took photos of each other, and everyone was just so damn happy about being in

Bourton.

Ben couldn't blame that at all as he rubbed the smooth soft hand of the man he might have been seriously falling for. There were hundreds of young and old families sitting on the grass banks of the shallow river watching their little kids go into the water to cool down or just splash around.

There were plenty of young and middle-aged topless men and women sun-bathing and Ben really enjoyed listening to everyone laugh, talk and giggle about the world around them.

Ben loved it here.

"This is beautiful," Ben said.

"Definitely," Max said as Ben laughed as Max was looking straight him at when he said that.

Ben kissed him quickly on the lips and he was certainly having the best time as they continued to slowly walk along the river. Smiling, waving and nodding their hellos to kids and parents as they ran after each other.

"What are your plans after uni?" Ben asked, not daring to even remotely mention he was moving to Australia. He just wanted to enjoy the moments he was having with Max without some massive departure and end hanging over them.

It was best.

"Before I met you I would have said I don't know, I would probably just hang around in the Cotswolds. But now, I really don't know. I need to explore,"

Ben hugged him a little tighter. "I wouldn't mind helping you out with that, there are tons of great places to explore. London, Bath, Canterbury to name a few,"

Ben loved it as Max smiled and his eyes widened with all those opportunities and Ben realised that he couldn't imagine being stuck in one place for a long time. Sure he had always grown up in Kent but he had still travelled, gone on holiday and explored the world a lot.

He was definitely going to call his parents later and thank them for giving him that privilege.

"But I wouldn't rush it," Ben said stepping to one side as a kid rushed past him. "Maybe just start with a day trip or something so you can get used to not being in the Cotswolds,"

Max playfully elbowed him in the ribs. "I'm not a complete newbie, I do know how to survive without my family and the Cotswolds,"

"Really?" Ben asked not wanting it to sound as serious as it came out.

Max pulled him closer to the edge of the water as they passed the last of the long line of sun-bathing tourists.

"Well no I haven't been anything before. I did go to Oxford a few times with my mates before and loved it. I had wanted to move there but that's when... well you know with mum,"

Ben hugged him tighter and they kissed a little.

They kissed a lot.

Ben tripped and they both screamed as they landed in the shallow river with the icy cold water running over them.

Ben smiled as a young family went past laughing and smiling at them.

"You know," Max said moving so close to his ear Ben could feel his wonderful breath on his skin, "if we go back out to the hills. We'll have to take our tops off for them to dry,"

"I like the way you think but I don't mind being wet around guys. I have seen ten ice cream men around here,"

Max shrugged. "Are you going to buy me one, city boy?"

Ben kissed his cheek. "Nope, you need to buy me one country boy. This is your village after all. Treat me and I might treat you later on,"

Max stood up and helped Ben up, not that he really needed it. Ben just wanted to touch Max for a little longer.

Ben watched as Max went over to the edge of the river bank, water dripping off his stunning curls before Max stopped and grinned at him.

"How are you going to treat me later?"

Ben knew it was just a joke between them at this point because he wasn't a *true* city boy. Canterbury wasn't as massive or powerful as places like London but Max didn't need to know that.

"I'll treat exactly how city boys treat other boys," Ben said grinning.

Ben laughed as Max mockingly hurried off to get him an ice cream and he couldn't deny he never ever wanted this to end.

Max was wonderful, kind and so cute and innocent, and Ben loved that a lot more than he ever wanted to admit even to himself.

# MEETING A COUNTRY MAN

# CHAPTER 12
20th May 2023

Bourton-On-The-Water, Cotswolds, England

Max was rather surprised as he held Ben's wonderful hand as they went back up the river past lots of great young families, hot men and women sunbathing and even more local people trying to sell rubbish to the tourists around them, that he had never ever had ice cream from the Cotswolds before.

Or at least how the tourists did.

Max held a large waffle cone of vegan vanilla ice cream in his hand and it was incredible, it was so refreshing, creamy and delicious. He had no idea something could ever taste this amazing and not contain a single animal product.

Sure he had had ice cream before from the village shop or something but his parents had always said that the ice cream sold to the tourists were always too commercial and imported to the area too much. It wasn't really natural or local as much as the tourist trappers said.

Max didn't care as he took one long lick of the amazing vanilla ice cream and it was like an explosive had gone off on his tongue. It made all tastebuds explode to life and it was the most luxurious thing he had ever tasted.

It was beyond incredible.

"You're acting like you're never had ice cream before," Ben said knowing how incredible it all was. "I've never had Cotswolds ice cream but I thought you would have,"

Max shrugged and stepped to one side as a dog rushed past with a panicked woman walking after it.

Ben laughed. "You have to love tourists,"

"God you sound like my dad sometimes," Max said grinning.

"He sounds like a wise man," Ben said and Max watched that tongue and mouth expertly work on his plant-based salted caramel ice cream that looked even more incredible than his vanilla.

"Please don't say that to him when you both meet,"

Ben stopped for a moment and smiled at him. "You think I'll meet your parents,"

Max went a little embarrassed and he wasn't sure if a drop of sweat rolled down his back or if it was still water from when they had fallen in the river.

"I don't know, maybe, only if you want," Max said failing to stay confident.

Ben nodded as three young women passed them

clearly checking them out. Max shook his head because he didn't want to mislead them in the slightest but he could understand that Ben just wanted to be polite.

"You like me a lot don't you?" Ben asked.

Max laughed and looked around to see if anyone was watching as they were coming up to a very small narrow alley in-between two large sandy yellow shops. He was fairly sure they were both tea rooms but Max didn't focus on so-called tourist traps so he wasn't sure.

When he knew the coast was clear he gently pulled Ben into the alley and they kept on walking until they weren't visible from people outside the alley.

Then Max pushed Ben against the wall and they both finished off their ice cream.

And Max kissed Ben. He made sure it was slow, tender and sweet and he made sure that it was perfect, caring and even a little loving.

Just to show how much he liked Ben and how much he cared about him. Ben was sweet, hot and there was just so much to him. It wasn't even that Ben had more life experience than him with Ben living in the city and travelling a lot more.

It was just that Ben was his ideal man in every way, and Ben cared about him. It was hard to find gay men in the Cotswolds and Oxford. Most were just looking for sex as they passed through and they were all young so they weren't looking for a relationship.

Something that Max really wanted himself, something he could hopefully have with Ben.

When he broke the kiss Ben smiled like a little schoolboy and Max loved it as Ben gently stoked away his long black curls from his face.

"You are so beautiful," Ben said.

Max grinned. his hands turned sweaty, his head went light and he couldn't believe he was actually having a great moment with such a hot man.

This was probably the first time he had ever done that before, he was actually having a real connection with a beautiful man.

A man he might even have been falling for.

"You know," Ben said slowly tracing a finger down Max's spine from the top to the very base of it, "we don't really have to never see each other after tomorrow. We could you know try a long distance thing for now and I could visit,"

"Or I could," Max said.

As soon as he said the words he took a few steps back, he was shocked that he had actually said he wanted to travel, leave the Cotswolds even for a short time and be away from his family.

It didn't feel weird, strange or bad. It actually felt amazing to want to leave this little slice of paradise and really start to see the world.

Ben took his hands in his. "Is that what you want to do?"

Max wasn't sure but whenever he was around Ben he didn't know what to think. He just felt so in lust, so calm and so great when he was around the man he really, really liked.

Ben made it seem like anything was possible.

"I'm more than okay," Max said giving the man he liked more than anything else in the world a massive kiss.

And Max couldn't deny how insanely happy he felt that he was going to have a long-term relationship after all.

Or was he?

# CHAPTER 13

20th May 2023

Bourton-On-The-Water, Cotswolds, England

As Ben and Max slowly went back towards Elliot's house in the late afternoon, Ben was surprised at how warm, toasty and relaxing the entire village was as the tourists were all mostly gone, the locals were heading out to the pubs for dinner and their evening pint and the air was so fresh.

Ben loved it here, but he loved it here with Max even more.

Ben waved at Quinn as she opened the pub for the evening bar shift that always started at 5 pm. He was a little surprised that she winked at *him* like he was some kind of saviour that had helped to save her little brother from something, and the massive white pub was a great building, really beautiful Cotswolds architecture and it just had a great feel to it.

That was something Ben was starting to notice more and more about the Cotswolds, there was just a feeling of love, relaxation and joy in the village that was something missing in the city. The city was still way, way better than the countryside but the countryside wasn't all bad

Ben had no idea how he had made the jump of really, really wanting to keep his relationship with Max as a summer fling to a real relationship. But when they were in the alley it was just so romantic, so sweet and so perfect that the words had just slipped out.

They really could be together forever if they could work out the one massive problem that Ben was really not looking forward to telling Max about.

But Ben was determined that tomorrow morning after Elliot's engagement party, he would come clean and tell Max about his move to Australia for his masters and he would move heaven and Earth to make sure their relationship would continue.

All because Ben truly believed in them and what their relationship was starting to turn into.

"What made you change your mind about travel?" Ben asked really hoping he could get Max to be more adventurous with his travel in the future.

"I think it's the idea and reward of seeing you," Max said knowing he needed to be more adventurous with his travel. "If I get to see you, be with you and get to explore with you then I think that's okay,"

"And I guess it seems less scary than exploring and travelling alone," Ben said.

"Exactly,"

Ben noticed Quinn was watching them through

the pub windows as she directed a group of tourists that were probably staying the night to an outside table.

"Why's your sister watching us so closely?" Ben asked.

Max laughed as he slowly guided Ben across one of the narrow tourist bridges that crossed the river so they could go straight up the road towards Elliot's house.

"Because I think she wants you to save me from this place,"

Ben slowly wrapped an arm around his sexy waist. "What's that meant to mean?"

"I guess until I met you I didn't know what it meant but now I think it means that there are no real opportunities in the Cotswolds. There aren't exactly many jobs, many education choices or many choices to find hot gay men so I think she wants me to move,"

"So you can find what you want to do in life and who you want to be with,"

"Exactly. All without being trapped in some Cotswolds village for the rest of my life,"

"Fair enough," Ben said pulling Max really close as he saw the top of Elliot's chimneys. "So tell me country man where do you want to go first?"

Ben could tell that Max was a little surprised at the question and he hadn't even thought about it.

"I don't know travel's new to me but I want to go. I want to explore England and I want to go traveling with you,"

Ben kissed him and he couldn't deny that he would love that. He loved the idea of him and Max walking hand in hand in London, Bath and York and so many other great places that would be stunning to visit.

It would be his ideal holiday and trip, he just wanted to spend time with a man that really, really liked him.

Max was definitely that person.

"London," Max said stopping in the middle of the road and wrapping his arms around Ben's neck. "I want to see London,"

"And we'll see it together," Ben said kissing Max's soft, insanely beautiful lips that he never ever wanted to part with.

After a few amazing moments Ben forced himself to break the kiss because they had a party to get to and he was so excited to finally be gay, be open and be in a relationship with the most stunning man he had ever met.

# CHAPTER 14
## 20th May 2023

Bourton-On-The-Water, Cotswolds, England

Later in the evening, Max wrapped his arms around Ben's wonderfully fit sexy body as everyone sat round a very large metal table in Elliot's massive garden. Max had always really liked the garden with its size, its rows upon rows of nice flower beds and the huge pine trees at the back.

But tonight the garden was simply perfect with everyone all around the table smiling, laughing and chatting away with each other.

Max seriously couldn't deny how stunning Ben was in his crisp white shirt and trousers that left nothing to the imagination, and Caleb and Hunter looked brilliant too. Max was surprised both men in their matching black jeans, blue shirts and shoes looked so good but they really did.

Max smiled at Elliot and Phillip in their black suits and they were almost as hot as Ben but Max was fairly sure that was impossible. Ben was just perfect and the entire afternoon had been beyond his wildest dreams. They had laughed so much, kissed so much and made so many plans for the future.

He couldn't believe he was planning to visit Canterbury in a few weeks and it had been his idea that they should become a couple, a real one and not a summer fling, something he was really happy Ben had said yes to.

Max kissed his boyfriend on the lips as he got up and went over to help a struggling Liz carry out two large trays of teas and coffees before they truly started on the alcohol. She looked lovely in her long white dress.

Hunter hissed as he declined yet another call from his girlfriend.

"And before anyone says anything I did call her," Hunter said.

Max leant forward. "Surely that must have sorted out everything?"

Ben laughed. It was such a beautiful sound Max knew he was never ever going to get tired of hearing it.

"I tried talking to her but she is just convinced about it now. She is so sure we'll break up that I... um, I just did it,"

No one dared speak and Max actually felt sorry for Hunter. He was such a good-looking, kind and caring guy that his girlfriend seriously didn't know what she was missing out on.

But Max understood why Hunter had done it, it was unfair on him that his girlfriend kept calling every single minute or every single day.

"I'm sorry mate," Ben said and Max could tell that he wanted to help and make things better for his best friend and that just made Max really like him even more.

"I'm looking forward to this food," Lucy said with a very subtle Australian accent not like she had been born there but she had certainly spent more than enough time there.

Max hadn't met Lucy before but he couldn't help but like her. She was so chilled, kind and she really did believe that everyone deserved a chance in life, even if it was a chance to get into yet another driving accident.

"I guess they don't have good cooks in a police station," Ben said and Max laughed as he sat back down.

Lucy shook her head. "No, no, no that isn't what happened. I was only late because I was driving slowly down the M25 to get here and then this monster truck teleported into the space in front of me,"

Max shook his head. He hadn't heard the full story yet so this was going to be good.

"So I slowed down but I broke too harshly so the idiot behind me smashed into me. Then the car smashed into his behind and the same happened for another three cars," Lucy said like it was nothing.

Max hugged Ben a little tighter. He was never

getting in a car with this woman.

"And then the police turned up all angry and blamed me, me of all people for what had happened. They arrested me, cleared the motorway up and they released me earlier today without any further action," Lucy said. "It was like magic,"

"Magic my ass," Liz said. "How much did you donate to the Police Orphanage Fund this time?"

Max laughed as Lucy looked offended.

"As if I would exactly pay two hundred thousand pounds to charity to avoid points on my license,"

"How can you afford *that* much money?" Max asked.

Everyone else around the table laughed minus Ben and Max felt like he was going to learn something massive.

"I'm a slightly successful business owner in Australia, New Zealand and the surrounding islands in the financial industry. If a business wants a partnership with another business or a loan I make it happen,"

"What was your turnover last year?" Liz asked clearly knowing the answer.

"That is top-secret business information that only my Aussie accountants need to know,"

"Was it two or four billion pounds?" Elliot asked.

Max was amazed and went close to his boyfriend. "Can you believe this? This is amazing. I love her,"

"Maybe you and me can visit someday. You

might as well explore the world properly by jumping in at the deep end,"

Max kissed Ben because that was a great idea, scary as hell but he wanted to travel, he wanted to see the world and he was starting to realised that Quinn was right. He did need to escape the Cotswolds before he was trapped here forever.

"I do like you, you know?" Ben asked. "Today's been amazing and the most fun I've had in ages. And who knew a country man could be so good at kissing?"

Max playfully hit him and gave him another quick kiss, and he just couldn't believe he finally had a boyfriend that he was going to go traveling with in a few weeks' time and more. They were going to have the best time together.

"So Lizzy tells me," Lucy said, "you finally got accepted into that Masters programme in Sydney. What wanna know mate about the land of Oz?"

Max just froze. What the hell was this about?

Ben froze too and Max wanted him to look at him but Ben wasn't moving a muscle.

"When does your Masters start?" Lucy asked clearly not catching on to what was happening.

Ben muttered something but Max couldn't hear.

"She didn't hear you," Max said icy cold.

It was only now he was realising what this could mean for their relationship or sheer lack thereof. Ben had lied to him from the beginning. There was never going to be a relationship, any love or anything more than a cheap fling.

"September," Ben said still not looking at Max.

Max just stood up and everyone just focused on them as they all realised what Ben had just confessed to.

Come September all the promises, kissing and nice words between them would mean nothing.

But most importantly Ben had lied to Max and Max was annoyed as hell.

# CHAPTER 15
## 20th May 2023
### Bourton-On-The-Water, Cotswolds, England

Ben flat out couldn't believe this was happening all he had wanted to do was wait until tomorrow morning to tell Max everything that was going on. He hadn't wanted Max to know about his move to Australia like this.

He looked at everyone at the table and they were all silent, frowning and they looked too scared to move.

Liz just looked at the floor and Hunter and Caleb didn't look like they knew what to do with themselves.

He smelt smoking, burning sausages from the kitchen but this was all way too bad for anyone to worry or even talk about food.

"What?" Max asked as he stood up.

Ben didn't know what to say, do or act. He wanted to run, he wanted to hug Max, he wanted to kiss him. He knew all of them were bad ideas.

"Why didn't you tell me you were moving to Australia? You said we were boyfriends, you said you wanted to go traveling. You said so many things. They were all lies!"

Ben went to hug him but Max backed away like he was diseased.

"No they weren't lies. I was going to tell you tomorrow. I want to be your boyfriend. I want to travel with you,"

"How could I go traveling with a liar? You still came some pretty epic secrets from me,"

"Yes I did and I am sorry but come on, we've only known each other two days," Ben said really hoping that calm things down.

Max laughed. "I was kidding myself then. All I wanted was a nice guy to kiss, like and maybe even have sex with. But you're just a typical city man tourist passing through. All you want is passion without anything real,"

Ben shook his head. "That isn't true. I'm not a liar, I didn't mean to mislead you or anything,"

Max looked at Elliot. "I'm sorry. I can't do this. You both look beautiful and at least Phillip never kept a massive secret like leaving the UK forever when you started dating,"

Elliot frowned. "Please let me get you a takeaway container of something. Take some food,"

Max went over and kissed Elliot on the cheek. "No thanks and have a good party. Congratulations on the engagement,"

"You don't have to leave," Ben said.

"Are you going then?" Max said sharply.

"No,"

"Then I will leave," Max said as he stormed off.

Ben looked at his friends and he couldn't read any of their expressions. This was all happening way too fast for him to understand.

Max clearly thought he had lied about wanting to travel with him, be with him and that he had simply been using a poor innocent country person with a little passion on a weekend away.

It wasn't a silly idea and Ben could understand why he thought that.

Ben ran after Max.

He found Max a little way down the long silent road when he caught up with him.

"Max please! I can explain! I really like you,"

Max stopped and shook his head. "If you really liked me, if you really respected me, if you gave a damn about me. Then you would have told me sooner,"

"I get that but-"

Max waved him silent and Ben noticed how wet his eyes were. "Do you not realise how much I liked you? How exciting and positive you were for me, a hot city man coming into the village and promising to help me explore beyond the Cotswolds?"

Ben shook his head. "I didn't. I'm sorry,"

"And you know what's worst? All my other so-called relationships have been this shallow before with city boys that wanna use me for sex. Or little village men in other places in the Cotswolds that don't want a real relationship because they're scared of what their village will think,"

Ben had no idea what to say, that was awful and those men were idiots.

"Am I an idiot or something? A loser that can't attract good men? So I just get all the liars and cheaters of the world,"

"No, you're amazing," Ben said.

Max shook his head like he didn't believe Ben. "Do you not realise how much courage and pain this caused me? I haven't left my family before, I haven't left the Cotswolds before and I was going to leave all of it including my mother and my pub duties just so I could see you from time to time,"

Ben gasped. He really hadn't thought about how much Max was willing to give up for him to try and make everything work between them.

"Clearly my feelings are too much so just leave and good luck in Australia. Maybe you'll find a guy you won't lie too,"

"But I want you," Ben said.

As Max started running down the road towards the family pub Ben just listened to him cry and he couldn't blame Max at all. He had said a lot of great things to him probably not a lot of guys had said those things to him but Max was so beautiful, so perfect and just Ben's ideal man that he couldn't believe this was happening.

Ben went over to a nearby flint wall, pressed his back against it as he sank to the floor and just buried his face in his knees.

And then allowed him the pain, anger and tears just flow out of him.

# CHAPTER 16
23rd May 2023

Bourton-On-The-Water, Cotswolds, England

Max still couldn't believe how dumb, stupid and pathetic he had been falling for Ben's charms, worldly knowledge and just his cheap tricks about being nice to him. He couldn't really deny that Ben probably hadn't meant to lie to him but it still happened.

Max had cried for the next day and a bit and he had even snapped at customers when the tourists were being stupid about the drinks or something. Normally he didn't care but the world just seemed darker than normal and the Cotswolds really were so small, silly and just boring after a while.

He hadn't realised that until now.

But right now he just had to focus on why his mother had got Quinn to fetch him for her when he was "happily" pulling pints for a cute gay tourist couple that said they were stopping in the pub before heading home.

At least they had each other but Max was still furious with them. Why did they get to be happy and he wasn't?

"Come in," his mother said as Max knocked at the heavy wooden door into her bedroom.

Max just smiled as he looked at his fragile mother sitting on her large Queen-size bed that barely fit into the ancient bedroom with its thick black beams shooting across the ceiling and Max was really glad all five of the bedroom windows were wide open today.

He would have hated his mother to be boiling away up here.

"How you feeling?" Max asked going over to her bedside and moving a large pile of his dad's crossword puzzles so he could sit down on a wooden chair.

"You know, the same really. The Cancer's going but it's the chemo that I think is killing me,"

Max held her hand. "Don't say that. The Chemo's healing you and you'll be fine in a few months,"

His mother looked like she was going to try and kiss his hand but she wasn't strong enough. She had only come back from the chemo appointment yesterday and Max had always hated those appointment days.

Max always hated the idea of his mother coming home crying because the doctors said the cancer was still spreading. Thankfully that wasn't going to happen.

"Why did you call me?" Max asked.

His mother weakly smiled. "Quinn and the regulars tell me you've been a, how I put this, *short* of late. You've snapped at your sister ten times in the past three days in private. You snapped at two tourist customers who only left happy because Quinn gave them a free drink and you insulted Mrs Brown's new dog,"

"That is not a dog that is a Yorkshire little rat pretending to be a dog. Oh, I get it now," Max said frowning.

His mother shook her head and Max hadn't even realised he had been taking out his anger on other people. He was just furious at Ben for making him believe that they were more than a summer or holiday fling, he wanted a relationship, he wanted to travel, he simply didn't want to be in the Cotswolds anymore.

"I am sorry you know," his mother said.

"For what?" Max asked having no idea what his mother was so sorry for. She had always been brilliant, amazing and wonderful to him.

"For not taking you and Quinn away on holiday at least once a year. It was never like we didn't have the money, we could have asked a friend to run the pub for us and yeah, I should have given you the opportunities me and your dad had,"

"What do you mean?" Max asked a little harsher than he wanted.

"Before me and your father were born, my grandparents died and they left us a lot of money. So we travelled around the entire world, visited all the cities in the UK and just saw it all,"

"Are you telling me? Me and Quinn grew up without going on holidays because you didn't want to revisit places,"

His mother didn't dare look at him. "Yes, we never took you anywhere because we loved the pub, we loved the Cotswolds and we… we made you believe you were needed here,"

Max shook his head. He couldn't believe this. This was beyond ridiculous.

"When you were younger and the pub was new and exciting we really did need you. But I was wrong to convince you to stay when you wanted to go to university in Cumbria or wherever you wanted to go,"

Max just stared at his mother. His entire life had been about helping out his parents, making sure he was close by to help them with the pub and just be with them when the cancer started.

Max had always been told that was what good sons did and he never wanted to disappoint his parents, but now it turned out they had lied to him. His parents had stopped him exploring the world, something he had completely forgotten he had wanted a few years ago.

"I could have had a normal university experience. I could have made university friends. I could have had relationships at university," Max said failing to keep the anger out of his voice. "But you stopped me from doing that,"

His mother leant forward smiling. "But I did it out of love because I love you and I don't want to lose you,"

Max laughed and he hugged her. "I'll always love you and Dad but I need to leave this place and just see the world,"

"You don't have any money. You don't have any idea about traveling,"

"There's the internet and I always save money from my wages and hell, I could get a job," Max said.

He went to walk out of the bedroom when his mother grabbed his arm.

"Just meet up with that man Quinn was telling me about. He can help you explore, travel, even make you realise who you are,"

Max wanted that so badly because he had always been a devoted country boy focused only on his family, he had never been anything else.

But he couldn't get back in contact with Ben, he was a liar and he was still leaving in September so he could spend the summer with him but then all the pain and agony and torture would start all over again in September.

There was no point.

But Max didn't want to be here anymore and as much as he wanted Ben, he simply couldn't let himself get hurt like that again.

# CHAPTER 17

24th May 2023

Canterbury, England

After days of trying to call beautiful, sexy Max, Ben just laid on the icy cold black leather chair in Liz's living room with his phone on his chest. He so badly wanted Max to pick up or call him back or answer a message but he was certain that Max had simply blocked him.

Ben listened to Liz, Hunter and Caleb talk about him on the sofas and armchairs, but he didn't pay attention. He wanted to fix it so badly, he wanted to do something, anything to show to Max just how much he meant to him.

The entire problem was that Max believed he was seeing him as a mere summer or holiday fling that was filled with promise but was always doomed to fail. Something Ben wanted to change but had no idea how to do it.

"You know," Liz said holding a mug of tea, "you

did promise that man a lot,"

Ben smiled at her. "You think I don't know that? How was I meant to know the man had never left the Cotswolds and this was a major, major step for him?"

"Because he said that to you," Hunter said.

"Shut up Hunter. Focus on your own problems," Ben said folding his arms hating that he had been such an idiot.

"Actually," Hunter said standing up and pretending to flex muscles he didn't have, "I don't have relationship problems anymore,"

Ben got up and hugged him. "That's incredible news,"

"Thanks mate," Hunter said. "Me and the girlfriend spent all night talking last night. And we agreed we were overreacting and we needed to start focusing on having each other rather than losing each other,"

Ben gave Hunter a little kiss on the cheek and he felt amazing. He felt like if Hunter and his girlfriend of all people could sort out their problems then maybe him and Max could too.

Something he wanted so, so badly.

Ben sat back down on the sofa and he looked at Caleb as his best friend looked like he wanted to say something but didn't know how to put it.

"Maybe he'll want to go with you?" Caleb said.

Ben sat up and folded his arms even more. He flat out hated all of this but he did love the idea of Max wanting to be with him, moving to another country with him and the two of them just being together.

"I would love," Ben said, "but moving to a new country on the other side of the world is tough enough for me. What about a man that has never left the Cotswolds?"

Liz nodded. "True, I doubt Australians ever know the word *village* considering they all mostly live around the south coast in monster cities,"

Ben rolled his eyes. He wanted a solution and it all seemed that the massive problem was the move to Australia.

"Maybe I shouldn't go," Ben said.

Everyone went silent and Ben picked up his large mug of coffee. He knew that it made sense because if he was staying in the UK then him and Max could be together, they could see each other more and they could go traveling around the UK together at weekends or something.

It would be perfect.

"But you worked so hard on everything to go to Australia," Liz said. "You did all that work for your Visa requirements and more,"

Ben nodded. That was a good point but Max was always more important to him.

Caleb leant forward. "Mate, are you saying you're going to change your entire future for a man that blocked you and doesn't want to talk to you?"

"Well anything in that tone would sound stupid," Ben said grinning.

Ben got up and paced around Liz's living room a few times. "Guys I know this seems crazy but I really like Max, there hasn't been an hour ever since I met him that I haven't thought about him,"

"Even when you were asleep?" Liz asked.

Ben just grinned because he really had had some extremely adult dreams about him and Max and what he wanted to do to his country boy.

Then Ben's hands turned sweaty, his head went really light and his stomach filled with butterflies. He realised that he didn't want to live in a world without Max, he wanted to wake up next to Max every day and he wanted to kiss Max goodnight every night.

"You love him don't you?" Liz asked.

"Damn it, I think I do," Ben said.

"Then what are you going to do about it?" Hunter asked grinning.

Ben looked at his best friends in the entire world. "I need to contact Sydney and kindly reject their offer, I need to apply for some UK unis and thankfully I know there'll still be spaces available. And most importantly I have to find Max,"

"You want to go to the Cotswolds?" Liz asked holding out her keys.

Ben shook his head. "Because I don't think he's going to be in the Cotswolds. I think he might be traveling or something. I need you guys to search social media, I'll phone Elliot and together I really hope we can find him,"

"Let's get to work," Liz said.

Ben really did love his friends but nowhere near as much as he loved his country man.

# CHAPTER 18
## 26th May 2023
## London, England

As much as Max really hadn't wanted Quinn to join him, he was glad that she had come as they both sat outside around a small black metal table on the street just outside a little café in the heart of Soho. Max was really impressed with how packed, loud and full of laughter the other rows upon rows of black outdoor tables were.

And he couldn't deny how much he loved it.

It was brilliant being around so many other people, so many other hot sexy men that had been winking at him all night and he was so looking forward to going to some gay clubs tonight. He just wanted to be free and experience what London's gay scene had to offer.

Quinn sipped her hot chocolate opposite him and grinned. "You're liking this trip then?"

Max nodded. He really had been enjoying it

because they had only gotten to London yesterday they had done so many cool things. He had visited the Houses of Parliament, got on the London Eye, gone on a river cruise of the River Thames and done so much more.

London was a brilliant place filled with great attractions and they were here until Sunday.

"Thanks for coming," Max said realising he was enjoying time with her. "And I'm sorry I snapped at you earlier in the week,"

Quinn gently took Max's hand in hers to the horror of some of the surrounding men on other tables.

"Relax guys I'm gay-only," Max said.

He laughed at some of the relieved faces on the other men.

"I'm proud that you finally realised that I was right all along and that you needed to get out of the Cotswolds,"

Max rolled his eyes. He hated his big sister being right and it was even worse that it was something as important as his future and what he wanted to do in life.

"What are your plans for tonight?" Max asked.

"I'm going to have a very adult night back in the hotel room with my laptop looking at jobs and cheap accommodation in the southeast,"

Max felt his stomach filled with butterflies at the idea of living in the same area of the country as Ben. They could visit, go out and continue their relationship.

Then Max realised that they couldn't because he was still going to Australia so Max would be traveling and living at last beyond the Cotswolds but he still wouldn't be with Ben.

The man he was fairly sure he was in love with at this point.

"Do you miss him?" Quinn asked.

Max took a small sip of his wonderfully smooth red wine. "Of course I miss him, I wanted him and I still want him,"

He was surprised that Quinn didn't say anything and she just wanted to listen, like she had always done to pub customers that needed to feel better. She really was an amazing sister.

"And I want him to realise that I really like him and we were right for each other. We were good together and that I want to explore the world with him,"

"Would you go to Australia?"

Max shrugged because he had no idea. This was the first time in his life he had ever left the Cotswolds and now his sister was talking about moving to Australia.

That was madness.

"I'll love you whatever happens and you still have your degree to fall back on," Quinn said getting up. "I just want another drink, want anything?"

Max shook his head as Quinn went off. He was almost certain a hot guy would slide into Quinn's chair and start flirting with him but no one did for now. He didn't know whether to be flattened or not.

He couldn't believe that Quinn had mentioned his fairly useless degree but he did love history and the conservation of historical ruins and it wasn't like Australia or any country was actually short on that work.

And it would be great to get some work experience in the field and then move on to a paid job.

Max just smiled because he couldn't believe that he was actually excited for the first time ever about his future, his job and he was finally realising he really could have anything he wanted in life.

If only he had Ben at his side.

Max took out his phone and he didn't go to Ben's phone number that he hadn't deleted yet, only blocked but he went onto his Online University Forum with all the other people in his cohort.

He smiled at how many people were messaging each other even now even though none of them had ever met, but some of the conversations sounded so personal that he knew he had missed out a ton on bonding with them.

He typed out a message. "Hi, sorry I haven't posted on here before but I want your help. My boyfriend's moving to Australia and I love him. I don't know if I should go with him because I've never left the Cotswolds before,"

He sent it and the entire group chat just stopped

then it started up with random people commenting.

"#LGBT+Students need help here," a student called Alice said.

"I know what you mean honey," a student called Cole said. "You need to do what's best for you, and what if it goes wrong in a new country?"

"It won't," Max said out of instinct and truly meaning it.

"Does he love you and want you to go with him?" Alice asked.

Max had no idea but he sort of knew that Ben would want him to be at his side all the time. "Yes of course he would,"

"Then what are you scared of?" Thomas asked.

Max had no idea who these random students were.

"I don't know," he wrote back, "I'm just scared and I want to be with him and I don't know what I'm feeling,"

"Have you spoken to him?" Alice asked.

Max laughed. "No because I blocked him after he... well he was a dick but I sort of forgive him now,"

Max shook his head as he finally realised that Ben wasn't an idiot for telling him about Australia, because Max knew, truly knew that Ben wasn't a horrible ugly guy that was nasty. He probably had meant to tell him the next day.

"But I overreacted," Max wrote, "and I need to talk to him straight away and just... tell him how I feel,"

"Log off then honey," Cole said. "Go and get your man,"

"Thanks everyone," Max said logging off.

Max was about to go and tell Quinn that he was going to grab a train down to Canterbury to see Ben when a very cute young man, the same age of him, sat down opposite him.

"Hi how it's going?" the hot man asked.

Max smiled and shook his head. "I'm sorry. I think you're a very hot guy and you are beautiful but I actually need to grab a train and rescue my relationship with my boyfriend. Um sorry,"

Max didn't even give the hot guy a chance to say anything as he simply rushed back to the nearest train station.

He would call Quinn but right now he just needed to get to Canterbury and fix everything.

But most of all he just needed, wanted Ben.

# CHAPTER 19
## 26th May 2023
### Canterbury, England

After two days of phoning people, searching the internet and looking around London last night for any signs of beautiful Max, Ben just couldn't find the man he really, really liked and probably loved.

He had sent Quinn over fifty messages but she hadn't replied to a single one and Ben couldn't blame her. Ben had hurt her little brother after all so maybe this was what he deserved and then some.

As Ben went along a small metal bridge that tried to make the entrance to his block flats at the university a lot posher than it really was, he couldn't help but realise this was probably the last time he would ever walk across here with a bag of shopping before he left in two weeks for home further up in Kent.

He focused on the large metal doors with floor-to-ceiling windows next to it, and it wasn't the most attractive of entrances but it did the job well enough. It was just a shame he hadn't done his job well enough to find the man he loved.

Ben leant against the cool metal railings of the bridge and just allowed the cool evening, almost night air wrap around him. There weren't many people on campus now that the exams were done and everyone was moving out.

All he wanted was to see Max again, to see his wonderful smile and just be with him.

"I hear you've been looking for me," Max said.

Ben jumped and laughed and cried as he saw the most beautiful man he had ever seen just standing there at the edge of the metal bridge. He was grinning like a little schoolboy and Ben couldn't believe how lucky he was.

He dropped his shopping and ran over to him.

Ben jumped up into the air and accidentally tackled Max to the ground as they hugged and kissed and Ben just brushed away Max's wonderful black curls.

"I've been searching everywhere for you. I went to London last night after I forced it out of Elliot," Ben said.

Max laughed. "I only just learnt how you've texting Quinn because she told me on the phone when I was on the train,"

Ben didn't get off him because he loved this moment, he loved seeing Max and he just loved being with him even if they were in a weird position in public.

"I'm not going to Australia anymore. I can get another Masters somewhere else, I just want to be with you and you alone,"

Max pulled him in for another kiss and Ben loved it. It was so soft, loving and tender.

"You're amazing but you didn't have to do that. We would have found a way to make it work, and my online degree's finished now anyway. I could have done it anywhere," Max said.

Ben shook his head. "I had to do it because no Masters, no degree, no anything is worth being away from you my little country man,"

Max laughed and hugged him. "You really are a city man aren't you? And I want to be with you so about we go upstairs, finally have sex and then tomorrow we can start to plan the future together,"

Ben loved it how his stomach filled with the butterflies at the idea of spending more precious time with such a hot country man and his wayward parts got excited about the idea of finally, finally having sex with such a perfect man.

And he had to admit as he gave Max another long, tender, loving kiss that it might have seemed weird that he had such strong feelings for Max only after a week together, but he hadn't lied the other day to his best friends. Ever since he had met Max there hadn't been a single hour or minute that he hadn't thought about him, his beauty and just how perfect he was.

"Let's go upstairs," Max said leading the way and Ben just laughed and kissed him all the way up to his flat and all the way to his bed.

# CHAPTER 20
## 23<sup>rd</sup> December 2023
### Paris, France

Max really loved his life as he looked out the large floor-to-ceiling windows of his and Ben's tiny little apartment in the heart of Paris near the university where they were both studying like crazy. Max couldn't deny how small and sometimes cramped it was with their bedroom being slightly smaller than his childhood bedroom in the Cotswolds and their bathroom being criminally small.

But Max loved it all.

Max was rather surprised how well he was picking up French and he had never realised he was good at languages before as he rested his head against the icy cold glass watching all the tourists, Parisians and mad Paris traffic drive up and down the immensely long street they were on.

Max couldn't believe how much he had changed in the last seven wonderful months with Ben. He was now more confident, happier and he was really loving life and he felt for the first time ever that he really did have friends. Not just at the university or at the gay bar that he worked at but also in Ben because they weren't just lovers or boyfriends, they were best friends.

He enjoyed the sweet aromas of pastries, rich bitter coffee and freshly baked French bread as the smell came in from the kitchen where Max had bought in fresh goods on the way home from the university to surprise Ben with.

He really hoped Ben would be home soon.

Max picked up his small white mug of coffee as he admired the tiny little living room that was barely large enough for their sofa, coffee table and bookshelves but he didn't care. The bookshelves were filled with cute photos of him and Ben together exploring, kissing and just being a couple.

They had visited the Rivera, they had got to Marseille and Normandy and everywhere in-between and none of it was bad. Max loved it that Quinn visited once a month as she now worked in London and was having the time of her life. And Max's mother was thankfully cancer-free and they had both decided that it was time to sell the pub off to a young couple they knew they could build a life here in the Cotswolds together and Max couldn't agree with that more.

His mother and father had all the money they needed for the rest of their lives so why not allow another gay couple in the area to make a great life out the pub? It really was perfect.

Max heard the front door go and he went over to the man he loved as he walked in with a shopping bag of his own and he placed his uni bag down and they exchanged long loving kisses even though they had only been apart for 8 hours.

Max gently led him over to the sofa and Max had to admit he would never ever get tired of looking at Ben's beautiful, handsome face.

"You are incredible you know that, right? I mean truly amazing," Ben asked.

Max pulled him close. "Only when you tell me that, but I just followed the man I loved wherever he wanted to do his Masters, and I'm just glad they accepted me on a French History course,"

"But you're more than that," Ben said kissing the man he loved. "You were a shy little country boy when we first met, you were scared about leaving the Cotswolds, your family and your pub. And now look at you, you're basically French and you're doing great in your course,"

Max smiled. It was always funny when he got better grades than the French natives did because some of them had been studying this stuff for years before him.

"And," Ben said getting down on one knee, "you are the most beautiful man I have ever met and you are the country boy I want to spend the rest of my life with. So would you Max Dillion do me the honour of becoming my husband?"

Max threw himself forward and he just kept kissing and grinding himself against Ben again and again. This was the most amazing thing anyone had ever done to him.

"Yes of course I'll marry you," Max said.

Ben laughed and they both started rolling around on the tiny floor together kissing and loving and enjoying each other.

And it was exactly then that Max realised that this was his life and his future and his dreams. He was finally going to have a real relationship, he was finally going to travel the world and escape the Cotswolds and most importantly he was finally going to be with a man that would love him, treasure and idolise him until death did them part.

And Max was going to do the exact same for Ben for the rest of time.

# CHAPTER 21
15th April 2024

Burton-On-The-Water, Cotswolds, England

Ben couldn't believe he was actually back in Bourton but it was great to be back in England after spending so long in wonderful France, and he was finally going to get married in front of friends and family and a whole ton of tourists because tourists season had clearly started earlier this year.

Ben sat in his black wedding suit inside Max's old family pub at one of the endless round wooden tables inside with Quinn sitting opposite him. The pub had definitely had a new lick of paint, the bar was new and everything was nice and shiny, but Ben still loved that it still felt old, cosy and definitely like it was from the last century. It was exactly what this village needed and it was good that the cute gay couple running it hadn't destroyed that character.

He was glad that Max had wanted to use it for their reception and it was actually big enough for all their English and French friends and family members to fit into it.

The air already smelt great with hints of juicy crispy pork, delightfully fresh French bread that Ben knew would melt into buttery deliciousness on the tongue and intensely flavourful roasted vegetables, that all left the taste of great French meals on his tongue.

Ben was so excited about today.

Him and Max had been planning the wedding so much, having sex even more when they got turned-on by a wedding joke or something and they had travelled most of France in search of wedding ideas.

And he had loved every single moment of it.

There wasn't a single man he had looked at in the past year and no one he would rather marry.

Ben looked at Quinn who was grinning at him. "You know I'm your family now?"

"I do and, I'm glad it's you," Quinn said. "And thank you to be honest for showing my brother that he needed to escape the Cotswolds, and in a way you helped me too. I never would have gone to London without you taking him away,"

Ben wanted to protest that he hadn't stolen her brother or anything, but he could tell that Quinn was truly happy about Max leaving and he didn't mind at all.

Everyone was thankfully happy, living their best life and really excited for today.

Quinn got up and hugged Ben tight. "I'm proud

to call you my brother,"

Ben felt a wave of emotion wash over him and he forced himself not to cry, not this early at least on his wedding day.

Liz, Caleb and Hunter came in and the two men had their girlfriends tightly on their arms. Ben got up and kissed Caleb and Hunter on the cheek, something the two girlfriends weren't a fan of but this was his wedding day and he was going to marry the love of his life.

"Congrats mate," Hunter and Caleb said. "We're really proud of you,"

"Thanks guys and congrats on your own engagements," Ben said spotting the golden rings on all their fingers.

Hunter's girlfriends smiled. "You could have waited until after Caleb had finished proposing,"

Hunter shrugged. "You would have married me anyway,"

"True," she said.

Ben smiled as Caleb and Hunter left with their girlfriends so they could take their seats along the river, because they wanted their wedding out in the wonderfully warm, refreshing Cotswolds air where everyone could see them.

"And you," Liz said hugging Ben tight, "are so lucky and I couldn't be happier for you,"

Ben hugged her back tightly and kissed her on the cheek. "You're my best friend, my favourite person and you are a sensational woman. And I want to come to your wedding one day,"

"When I meet an Aussie man I'll tell you I promise," Liz said walking off to get to her seat.

Ben was so pleased for Liz that she had joined Lucy's company out in Australia and thankfully she was having the time of her life making new friends, meeting new men and just living life.

Because if his relationship and love and passion with Max had taught him anything, it was that Ben now truly knew that life was too short to stay inside a comfort zone. The world was a massive place and it needed to be experienced, enjoyed and taken advantage of because no one could be a city man or country man forever. The two always had to mix.

And as he heard the music change outside, Ben stood up and hooked an arm with Quinn as they both went out of the pub and up the isle towards Max, the man he loved more than anything, the man he would always treasure and the man that Ben knew he was so damn lucky to be getting married too.

And spending the rest of his life with him.

The very definition of a perfectly happy life and Ben was still surprised that all it had taken for him to find true love and happiness was for him to meet a country man.

GET YOUR FREE SHORT STORY NOW!
And get signed up to Connor Whiteley's
newsletter to hear about new gripping books,
offers and exciting projects. (You'll never be
sent spam)

https://www.subscribepage.io/gayromancesig
nup

About the author:

Connor Whiteley is the author of over 60 books in the sci-fi fantasy, nonfiction psychology and books for writer's genre and he is a Human Branding Speaker and Consultant.

He is a passionate warhammer 40,000 reader, psychology student and author.

Who narrates his own audiobooks and he hosts The Psychology World Podcast.

All whilst studying Psychology at the University of Kent, England.

Also, he was a former Explorer Scout where he gave a speech to the Maltese President in August 2018 and he attended Prince Charles' 70th Birthday Party at Buckingham Palace in May 2018.

Plus, he is a self-confessed coffee lover!

Other books by Connor Whiteley:
Bettie English Private Eye Series
A Very Private Woman
The Russian Case
A Very Urgent Matter
A Case Most Personal
Trains, Scots and Private Eyes
The Federation Protects
Cops, Robbers and Private Eyes
Just Ask Bettie English
An Inheritance To Die For
The Death of Graham Adams
Bearing Witness
The Twelve
The Wrong Body
The Assassination Of Bettie English
Wining And Dying
Eight Hours
Uniformed Cabal
A Case Most Christmas

Gay Romance Novellas
Breaking, Nursing, Repairing A Broken Heart
Jacob And Daniel
Fallen For A Lie
Spying And Weddings
Clean Break

Awakening Love
Meeting A Country Man
Loving Prime Minister
Snowed In Love
Never Been Kissed
Love Betrays You

Lord of War Origin Trilogy:
Not Scared Of The Dark
Madness
Burn Them All

The Fireheart Fantasy Series
Heart of Fire
Heart of Lies
Heart of Prophecy
Heart of Bones
Heart of Fate

City of Assassins (Urban Fantasy)
City of Death
City of Martyrs
City of Pleasure
City of Power

<u>Agents of The Emperor</u>
Return of The Ancient Ones
Vigilance
Angels of Fire
Kingmaker
The Eight
The Lost Generation
Hunt
Emperor's Council
Speaker of Treachery
Birth Of The Empire
Terraforma
Spaceguard

<u>The Rising Augusta Fantasy Adventure Series</u>
Rise To Power
Rising Walls
Rising Force
Rising Realm

<u>Lord Of War Trilogy (Agents of The Emperor)</u>
Not Scared Of The Dark
Madness
Burn It All Down

Miscellaneous:
RETURN
FREEDOM
SALVATION
Reflection of Mount Flame
The Masked One
The Great Deer
English Independence

## OTHER SHORT STORIES BY CONNOR WHITELEY

Mystery Short Story Collections

Criminally Good Stories Volume 1: 20 Detective Mystery Short Stories

Criminally Good Stories Volume 2: 20 Private Investigator Short Stories

Criminally Good Stories Volume 3: 20 Crime Fiction Short Stories

Criminally Good Stories Volume 4: 20 Science Fiction and Fantasy Mystery Short Stories

Criminally Good Stories Volume 5: 20 Romantic Suspense Short Stories

Mystery Short Stories:
Protecting The Woman She Hated
Finding A Royal Friend
Our Woman In Paris
Corrupt Driving
A Prime Assassination
Jubilee Thief
Jubilee, Terror, Celebrations
Negative Jubilation
Ghostly Jubilation
Killing For Womenkind
A Snowy Death
Miracle Of Death
A Spy In Rome
The 12:30 To St Pancreas
A Country In Trouble
A Smokey Way To Go
A Spicy Way To GO
A Marketing Way To Go
A Missing Way To Go
A Showering Way To Go
Poison In The Candy Cane
Kendra Detective Mystery Collection Volume 1
Kendra Detective Mystery Collection Volume 2
Mystery Short Story Collection Volume 1

Mystery Short Story Collection Volume 2
Criminal Performance
Candy Detectives
Key To Birth In The Past

Science Fiction Short Stories:
Their Brave New World
Gummy Bear Detective
The Candy Detective
What Candies Fear
The Blurred Image
Shattered Legions
The First Rememberer
Life of A Rememberer
System of Wonder
Lifesaver
Remarkable Way She Died
The Interrogation of Annabella Stormic
Blade of The Emperor
Arbiter's Truth
Computation of Battle
Old One's Wrath
Puppets and Masters
Ship of Plague
Interrogation
Edge of Failure